The Ugly Duckling

By HANS CHRISTIAN ANDERSEN

Illustrated by
ROBERT VAN NUTT

ALFRED A. KNOPF PUBLISHERS • NEW YORK

This is a Borzoi Book published by Alfred A. Knopf, Inc.

Published in the United States by Alfred A. Knopf, Inc., New York,
and simultaneously in Canada by Random House of Canada Limited,
Toronto. Distributed by Random House, Inc., New York.

MANUFACTURED IN THE UNITED STATES OF AMERICA

Designed by Antler & Baldwin Design Group

2   4   6   8   10   9   7   5   3   1

Library of Congress Cataloging-in-Publication Data
Andersen, H. C. (Hans Christian), 1805–1875. The ugly duckling.
Translation of: Den grimme ælling.
Summary: An ugly duckling spends an unhappy year ostracized by the other
animals before he grows into a beautiful swan.
[1. Fairy tales] I. Van Nutt, Robert, ill. II. Title.
PZ8.A542Ug   1986b   [Fic]   86-185
ISBN 0-394-88403-5   ISBN 0-394-88298-9 (book/cassette)

*As adapted by Joel Tuber and Clara Stites for
the video version of THE UGLY DUCKLING
narrated by Cher
directed by Mark Sottnick*

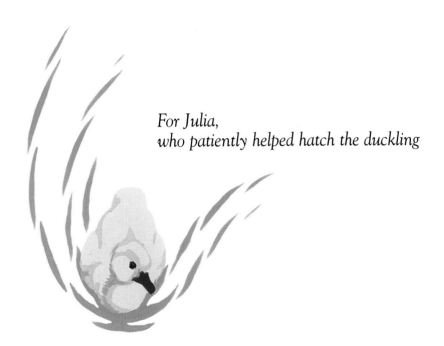

For Julia,
who patiently helped hatch the duckling

The long golden days of summer had come to the countryside. The air was sweet, the corn stood tall and green, and row upon row of freshly cut hay lay drying in the meadows.

Beyond the open fields, forests of tall, silent trees shaded deep, cool lakes. Storks strutted through the marshes on their long red legs, and little birds flew overhead chattering.

On a hilltop bathed in sunshine stood an old mansion surrounded by a moat. Along the stone walls of the moat huge burdock plants with leaves as big as platters grew thick and tall. Beneath their leaves it was like a secret room.

A mother duck had made her nest, and she sat waiting for her eggs to hatch. She had been sitting a long time, or so it seemed to her, and she missed the company of all the other ducks. But she knew that soon she would have a brood of lively ducklings to watch over, and so she sat patiently on her nest beneath the burdock leaves.

At last the eggs began to crack, and from each emerged a clumsy little duckling all damp and unsteady on big webbed feet. In no time at all their feathers dried, and they looked like little yellow puffs as they scuttled about.

"Quack, quack," said the mother duck. "Peep, peep," the ducklings answered as they stared at their leafy green shelter. Their mother let them look as much as they liked, for green is good for the eyes.

"How big the world is," peeped the ducklings, shaking out their tiny wings and enjoying the freedom they now had outside their eggs.

"Oh, my little sillies. Do you suppose that this is all there is to the world? Why, it stretches way beyond the other side of the garden. Though I have never been that far myself."

The mother duck counted her children. "You are all here now, aren't you?" Then she got up from her nest. "No, you are not all here. There is still one egg unhatched, and it is the biggest egg of all. Oh, I am so tired of waiting!" But then she settled back down to keep the last egg warm beneath her feathers.

Just then an old duck came by to say good morning. "Well, how are you doing?" she asked.

"Look at my children," said the mother duck proudly. "Aren't they the finest ducklings you have ever seen? Though my last one is taking such a long time to hatch."

"Let's see that egg," said the old duck. "Ah, that's a turkey egg for certain. I know because the same trick was once played on me—and such trouble I had. The foolish young turkey was afraid of the water. And try as I might, I could not get him to swim. I begged and I scolded, but it was no use." The old duck shook her head. "Yes, I am sure that's a turkey's egg. If I were you, I would let it be and teach my *real* ducklings how to swim."

"But I've already waited so long," said the mother duck. "I may as well wait a little longer."

"Well," said the old duck, "please yourself . . . "

That evening the egg began to tremble. Then it cracked open, and with a "Cheep! Cheep!" out tumbled the last duckling.

Just like the others, he quickly shook his feathers dry and grew steady on his feet. But how big he was! And all gray. And compared to the other ducklings, how ugly!

The mother duck just looked at him. "Can he be a turkey chick after all?" she wondered. "Well, we'll soon find out. Into the water he'll go, even if I have to push him in myself."

The next day was sunny and bright. The mother duck took her family down to the moat. Splash! In she went. "Quack, quack," she called. And splash! splash! splash! one after another, the ducklings jumped in after her. The water went way up over their heads, but in a moment they rose to the surface where they floated beautifully.

"That's no turkey," thought the mother duck. "Just look how well he uses his legs and how straight he holds himself. He is my own child after all, and really not so ugly when you look at him properly."

"Come along, children. Let me introduce you to the barnyard. But take care to stay close to me, and watch out for that mean old cat."

The mother duck led her ducklings into the poultry yard, where a great commotion was going on. Two families of geese were squabbling, hissing and snapping their beaks at one another.

"That is what the world is like," said the mother duck. "Hurry along now, children, and don't turn your toes in! A well-bred duck walks with toes out, like this." And she waddled along, her ducklings following in a row.

"Be sure to bow to the old duck over there. She is the most distinguished resident of the barnyard. Her ancestors came all the way from China. And see that bit of red cloth on her leg? It means that everyone is to take notice of her and treat her with respect. Make a bow, then, and say quack."

The ducklings did as they were told, but the barnyard chickens upon seeing them said rather loudly, "Humph! Now we shall have to make room for *that* mob. As if there weren't enough of us already. And my goodness! What an odd-looking fellow that last one is! We certainly don't want him around here!"

And one of the chickens flew right at the ugly duckling and bit him on the neck.

"Leave him alone!" cried the mother duck. "He's doing no harm."

"But he's so big and gawky," said one chicken.

"And peculiar looking," said another. "He doesn't belong here."

Then the old China duck spoke up. "That is a fine family. All the children are pretty—except for that gray one. Too bad you can't start over again with him."

"That can't be done, Your Grace. I know he isn't handsome. He stayed too long inside the egg, and that has spoiled his shape. But he is good-tempered and he swims as well as all the others. And I am sure he will turn out all right."

But that was only the first day. After that the ugly duckling's troubles grew worse. Everyone chased him and made fun of him. Even his own brothers and sisters were cruel. "You are so ugly," they said. "The cat should grab you." And the mother duck looked at him sadly and wished he were far away. The ducks snapped at him, and the hens pecked at him, and even the girl who brought the feed kicked him aside with her foot.

Early one morning the duckling decided to run away. He scurried under the fence, so startling the wild birds who roosted in the bushes that they flew into the air crying.

"They are afraid of me because I am so ugly," the duckling thought as he struggled across the meadow.

At last he reached the great marsh where the wild ducks lived. He hid himself among the reeds and lay there all night, exhausted and alone.

In the morning the wild ducks flew over to him. "What sort of creature are you?" they asked.

The duckling greeted them as politely as he knew how. "I am a duckling."

"What a strange-looking one you are! But that won't matter to us as long as you don't marry into our family." With a great flutter of wings the wild ducks flew away.

The poor little duckling had no thought of marrying. He only wanted a quiet place to rest and a little water to drink. For two whole days he stayed in the marsh and no one bothered him.

Then one morning he was visited by a pair of wild geese. They were very lively and talkative. "Listen, friend. Why don't you come with us to the other side of the marsh, where all the wild geese live. They are so pretty that ugly as you are, they might like you."

The two young geese turned to lead the way when bang! bang! Shots suddenly rang out above them.

Bang! bang! sounded again, and a great flock of wild geese flew up from the rushes. The hunters were everywhere, even in the trees overhanging the reeds.

The smoke from their guns rose in the air. Then the dogs came splashing through the marsh. The poor duckling was terrified, and he was about to hide his head under his wing when a huge dog was upon him. Its great tongue hung out of its mouth; its eyes gleamed horribly. It pushed its nose right into the face of the duckling. Then off it went.

"I'm so ugly even the dog doesn't want me," thought the duckling. And he lay very still while the gunshots echoed across the marsh.

It was late in the day before the shooting stopped. But it was a long time before the duckling dared move. Then he slowly raised his head and looked around. All was still. He hurried away from the marsh as fast as he could.

Toward evening he came to a sad-looking little farmhouse. Inside lived an old woman, a cat, and a hen. The cat could arch his back and purr. He could also give off sparks if his fur was rubbed the wrong way. The hen laid many eggs, and the old woman loved her as if she were her own child.

When daylight came, the old woman, the cat, and the hen woke up and discovered the stranger in their house. The cat began to purr and the hen to cluck.

The old woman, whose eyes were not good, thought the duckling was a full-grown bird. "What a lucky find! Now I can have duck eggs."

So the duckling was allowed to stay there for three weeks, but of course, no eggs appeared. The cat and the hen looked down their noses at the duckling. When the duckling tried to start a conversation with them the hen would say, "Can you lay eggs?"

"No."

"Well then, you have nothing to say to me!"

The cat would ask, "Can you arch your back or purr?"

"No."

"Well then, keep your opinions to yourself."

So the duckling sat in the corner feeling very, very sad. Thoughts of fresh air and sunshine came to his mind, and he was filled with an extraordinary longing to swim.

But when he dared mention it to the hen, she was scornful. "What a preposterous notion! The trouble with you is that you have nothing to keep you busy. Try laying a few eggs, or practicing your purring. Soon you'll forget about such silly longings."

"But it is so wonderful to swim, and to feel the water rushing up over your head when you dive to the bottom."

"You must be crazy!" said the hen. "Ask the cat about it. He's the cleverest creature I know. Ask him if he is fond of swimming or diving under the water. Ask the old woman—she is the wisest mistress in the world. Do you think she has any desire to swim or dive?"

"You don't understand," said the duckling.

"If we don't understand, I'd like to know who does," said the cat. "You'll never be as wise or clever as we are. Don't be foolish. Give thanks for all the kindness you have met with here. You have found a warm room and pleasant company. You might even learn something from us if only you'd listen. But no—all you do is talk nonsense. Now try to be more cheerful, and lay a few eggs."

"I think I had better go out into the wide world," said the duckling.

"Well then, go!" said the hen.

So the duckling went. He did not have too far to go before he found a beautiful pond. He swam and he dived, but whenever he tried to swim near the other ducks, they turned away from him because he was so ugly.

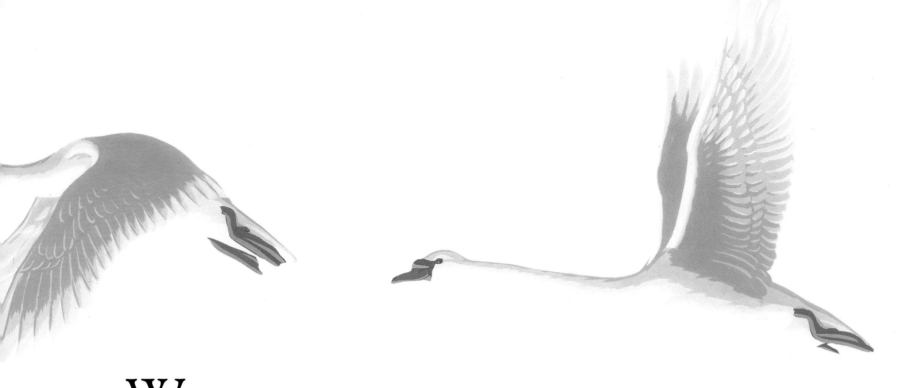

Winter was coming. The leaves had fallen from the trees, the air was frosty, and the clouds hung heavy with snow. A raven perched on the fence squawked "Caw! Caw!" because it was so cold. It was a very difficult time for the lonely duckling.

One evening as the setting sun colored the sky, a flock of large, handsome birds appeared. The duckling had never seen anything so beautiful. The birds were dazzling white and had long graceful necks. They circled high in the air, and the little duckling felt strangely excited as he watched them. He swam round and round in circles and called out to them in a voice so loud and so shrill it frightened him.

He watched till the last one was gone from sight. Then he dived straight down to the bottom of the pond. When he came up again, he was even more excited than before. He did not know what the birds were or where they flew, but he felt drawn to them more strongly than to anything he had ever known before. Oh, he would never forget those wonderful white birds!

The winter grew bitterly cold. The duckling had to swim round and round in the water to keep it from freezing right up. But every night the pool in which he swam grew smaller and smaller.

Then one night the ice froze so solid you could hear it creaking, and the duckling was so cold and so weary he could no longer move. At last he froze fast into the pond.

Early next morning a peasant passing by saw the duckling. He broke up the ice with his wooden clog and carried the little duckling home to his wife. In the warm house they revived him.

The children wanted to play with him, but the duckling was afraid they might hurt him and he fluttered away. In a panic he flew right into the milk pan.

The wife screamed and waved her apron at him, and he flew into the butter tub, and from there into the flour barrel. What a sight he was!

It was a good thing the door was open. The duckling darted out into the bushes, where he lay exhausted in the new-fallen snow.

The poor duckling dragged himself to the reeds at the edge of the frozen pond, where he found a few meager grains to eat and scant shelter from the brutal winds.

It would be much too sad to tell you of the misery and hardships the duckling had to endure that long, cold winter.

Spring finally came again to the countryside. The duckling woke to find the sky bright and the larks singing. He tried his wings. They were stronger than before and they carried him swiftly away.

Before he knew it, he found himself in a large garden where apple trees blossomed and sweet-smelling lilacs dangled their long branches over the waters of a lake. Right ahead of him, out of the leafy shadows, came three beautiful white swans. With their elegant heads held high, they glided lightly across the water.

The duckling recognized the splendid birds and was overcome by a strange sadness. "I will fly to them even though they will peck me to death because I am so ugly. Better to be killed by such lovely creatures than to be scoffed at by ducks and hens and kicked by serving girls. Better to die now than endure another cold, hard winter." So he swam out to meet the swans.

They came towards him with ruffled feathers. The poor duckling bowed his head down to the water.

But what did he see in the water?

His own reflection. He was himself a swan!

It did not matter that he was born in a duck's nest. He was hatched from a swan's egg!

The three lovely swans circled round and round and stroked him gently with their beaks. Some little children came into the garden and threw bits of bread into the water for the birds. Then the smallest child cried out, "Look! A new swan! The new one is the prettiest one of all."

The old swans bowed their heads in agreement. This made the duckling feel quite shy, and he tucked his head under his wing. He was very, very happy and not proud at all, for a good heart is never proud.

The lilacs bent their branches down to the water to greet him, and the bright sun shone on him. His heart filled with joy, and he ruffled his feathers and raised his slender neck, for he had never dreamed of so much happiness when he was an ugly duckling.